Fergus the Friendly Puppy

As soon as the car had stopped outside the house, the front door opened and Fergus shot out barking loudly.

He saw Alison and woofed a hello at her. Alison nodded and managed a smile, but said nothing.

Fergus stared at her in shock. His tail stopped wagging. Didn't Alison *want* to be his friend?

Titles in Jenny Dale's PUPPY TALES™ series

1. Gus the Greedy Puppy
2. Lily the Lost Puppy
3. Spot the Sporty Puppy
4. Lenny the Lazy Puppy
5. Max the Mucky Puppy
6. Billy the Brave Puppy
7. Nipper the Noisy Puppy
8. Tilly the Tidy Puppy
9. Spike the Special Puppy
10. Hattie the Homeless Puppy
11. Merlin the Magic Puppy
12. Fergus the Friendly Puppy

All of Jenny Dale's PUPPY TALES books can be ordered at your local bookshop or are available by post from Book Service by Post (tel: 01624 675137)

Jenny Dale's
PUPPY
TALES™

Fergus the Friendly
Puppy

by Jenny Dale

Illustrated by Susan Hellard

A Working Partners Book

MACMILLAN CHILDREN'S BOOKS

To the real Mary Grice and her three wonderful

daughters – Lauren, Alison and Sarah

Special thanks to Narinder Dhami

First published 2000 by Macmillan Children's Books
a division of Macmillan Publishers Limited
25 Eccleston Place, London SW1W 9NF
Basingstoke and Oxford
www.macmillan.co.uk

Associated companies throughout the world

Created by Working Partners Limited
London W6 0QT

ISBN 0 330 48105 3

A CIP catalogue record for this book is available from
the British Library.

Typeset by SX Composing DTP, Rayleigh, Essex
Printed and bound in Great Britain by Mackays of Chatham plc, Kent

Chapter One

"I know who that is!" Fergus
barked happily as the doorbell
rang. "It's my friend the postman!"
   The puppy leaped to his feet
and charged towards the front
door, barking loudly. "Hold on,
Mr Postman! Rod's coming to
open the door."

"Quiet, Fergus!" called Rod, Fergus's owner. He got up from his computer and ran after the excited puppy. "Now just calm down!"

"But it's my friend the postman!" Fergus barked, as he scrabbled frantically at the front door. "Quick, I want to say hello!"

Rod laughed, and scooped the Bernese Mountain pup into his arms. "Don't lick him to death now, Fergus!" he teased.

The postman was standing outside with a large envelope in his hand, looking rather nervous.

"Hey, that's not *our* postman!" Fergus woofed, getting even more excited. "This is a *new* postman." And he began to wriggle

impatiently in Rod's arms. "Put me down, Rod."

"Are you Mr Ritchie?" the postman asked, keeping a wary eye on Fergus. "You need to sign for this letter."

"OK," Rod nodded. "You don't mind if I put Fergus down, do you? He won't hurt you."

The postman looked at the large and strong-looking black-and-tan pup. "He seems a bit excited," he muttered. "Are you sure he won't attack me?"

"Fergus? You must be joking!" Rod laughed, putting the puppy down. "He just wants to be everyone's friend."

"Free at last!" Fergus barked happily. "Now, let's really get to know each other." He snuffled round the postman's trainers for a moment or two, and then jumped up at him, as Rod signed for the letter.

"I hope all the dogs I meet on my new round are as friendly as you," the postman said, patting Fergus gingerly on the head.

"Watch out for the bulldog at Number 10!" Fergus woofed. "He's not friendly at all!"

"Right, Fergus, I'm just going to read my letters," Rod said, as he closed the door. "Then we'll go to the park, OK?"

Snuffling happily, Fergus padded back into the study behind his owner. He liked making friends with everyone, but Rod was his *best* friend.

Rod had a big house and garden, and he really loved animals. Besides Fergus, there was a large tank of tropical fish in the living room, as well as an aviary of brightly coloured birds in the garden. Best of all, Rod worked at home on his computer,

so he was with Fergus every day.
Fergus had heard some of his
doggy friends complaining about
how bored they were while their
owners were out at work.

Yes, I am a very *lucky puppy,*
Fergus thought, as he chewed on
a rubber bone. "Are you almost
ready to go to the park, Rod?" he
barked.

"Quiet, Fergus," Rod said.

The puppy glanced up at his
owner. He saw that Rod was
frowning as he read one of his
letters. Fergus wondered why.

Then Rod put the letter down,
and picked up the phone. Fergus
knew that Rod didn't like him to
make a noise when he was talking
to someone, so he sat quietly, not

even wagging his tail.

"Hello, Mary?" Rod smiled as he spoke into the receiver. "It's me. I didn't get you out of bed, did I? Oh, good."

Fergus pricked up his ears. He didn't know who Mary was, but maybe she was going to be a new friend.

"The thing is," Rod went on, "I've just had a letter offering me a really good computer job in America. It's only for a month, but I need someone to look after the house and my pets while I'm away."

Fergus was shocked. Rod was going away? He couldn't help whining miserably. Fergus didn't know what or where America was, but he certainly didn't want his owner to be away from home – for even one day!

"So I was wondering if you and the girls would like to come and stay," Rod said, as he bent down to stroke Fergus's silky ears. "I know their summer holidays are coming up."

Fergus stopped whining, and pricked up his ears again. Maybe it wouldn't be *so* bad if there was someone else to look after him . . .

"That's great!" Rod sounded much happier now. "I really appreciate it, Mary," he said. "Sorry it's such short notice. Oh, and by the way, I've got a puppy now. He's called Fergus, and the girls are going to love him!"

Fergus wondered who "the girls" were. It sounded like *lots* of people were going to come and look after him.

"Bye, and thanks again." Rod put the phone down, and turned to Fergus with a smile. "Now I won't have to worry about anything while I'm away," he said. "My sister Mary is going to move in and look after you. She's a writer, so she'll be able to work here on my computer, and my three nieces, Lauren, Alison and Sarah, are coming too."

Fergus cheered up and wagged his tail a little. After all, Rod wouldn't be away for ever, and he'd made sure that Fergus would be well looked after.

Fergus just couldn't *wait* to meet all his new friends!

Chapter Two

"Are we nearly there yet, Mum?"
Lauren Grice asked impatiently,
from the back seat.

"It's just a few more miles,
thank goodness!" Mrs Grice
replied, as she drove along the
country road. "I know it was a
long journey, girls, but you've all

been very good."

"I can't wait to see Uncle Rod's house!" Sarah bounced up and down in the front passenger seat. "I've never been to it before."

"Yes, you have, but you were only a baby," her mother replied. "You probably don't remember."

"Sarah's *still* a baby!" Lauren said, grinning.

"No, I'm not, I'm five!" Sarah turned round and thumped her eldest sister on the only bit she could reach – Lauren's knee.

"Stop it, you two," Mrs Grice said firmly. She drew to a halt at some traffic lights and looked at her watch. "I'm glad we're on time," she said. "Your uncle Rod has to leave in a couple of hours to catch his plane."

"I want to see Gerfus the puppy!" said Sarah eagerly.

"Not Gerfus – Fergus!" Lauren corrected her, in fits of laughter.

"That's what I said," Sarah sniffed.

"Are you all right, Ali?" Mrs Grice glanced in her mirror at the back seat, where eight-year-old Alison was sitting with Lauren. "You're very quiet."

"I'm fine," Alison said. But she wasn't fine at all. She had been looking forward to the school holidays at home, and now they were going to stay in a strange place for four whole weeks.

Alison couldn't even remember Uncle Rod very well. He'd

worked abroad for a long time, and so he hadn't visited them much. Besides, Alison was very shy and she didn't like new places or new people very much.

As the car slowed down at a junction, Lauren called out, "Oh, look! There's a car boot sale on Sunday. Can we go, Mum?"

Mrs Grice smiled. "I should think so," she said. Then she looked at Alison in her rear-view mirror. "That might cheer you up a bit, love."

Alison gave a little smile back. They all liked hunting round car boot sales.

"Here we are!" Mrs Grice said half an hour later, as she turned the car into the driveway of her brother's house. Lauren and Sarah both started bouncing up and down in their seats with excitement, but Alison felt even more miserable.

As soon as the car had stopped, the front door opened. A bundle of black-and-tan fur shot out, barking loudly, followed by Uncle Rod.

"Oh, look at the puppy!" Sarah squealed. "It's Gerfus – I mean, Fergus!"

"I want to hold him!" Lauren was already struggling to undo her seat belt.

"No, me first!" Sarah wailed.

"I can see who's the popular one around here!" Rod laughed, as he

gave his sister a kiss. "Great to see you, Mary. Did you have a good journey?"

Meanwhile, Fergus had leaped into Lauren's arms, and was busy covering *her* face with kisses.

"Oh, he's lovely!" Lauren laughed, bending down so that Sarah could stroke him too.

"Hello! I'm your new friend!"

Fergus snuffled, giving Sarah a sloppy kiss too.

He was so busy being fussed over by the others that at first he didn't notice that there was someone else in the car. Then he saw Alison getting out, and woofed, "Hello, I'm Fergus! Let's be friends!"

"Isn't he gorgeous, Ali?" Lauren asked, rubbing her face against the puppy's soft fur.

Alison nodded and managed a smile, but said nothing.

Fergus stared at her, feeling quite shocked. His tail stopped wagging. Didn't Alison *want* to be his friend?

"Come in, and I'll show you to your rooms," Rod said, as he

helped Mrs Grice unload their bags from the car. "I've put you all in separate bedrooms, but the girls can share if they want to."

"No, thank you!" Lauren and Alison said quickly.

As everyone went upstairs, Fergus raced ahead. But he kept looking back at Alison. She didn't look very happy to be there at all.

That made Fergus a bit miserable too. He wanted *everyone* to be happy.

"This is your room, Lauren," Rod said, as he opened the nearest door. "And this is yours, Alison," he added, moving to the next door along. "Sarah, you and your mum are next to each other, over here . . ."

"Oh, this is great!" Lauren gasped, as she went into her bedroom. "This is bigger than my room at home, and I have to share that with Ali."

Fergus padded along to Alison's room and followed her in.

Alison went and sat on her bed, looking as if she was about to cry.

Alarmed, Fergus rushed over to

her, and began to paw at her legs. "Don't be sad, Alison," he woofed. "It's great here!"

Alison looked down into the puppy's big, brown eyes, and couldn't help smiling. She bent down to stroke his silky ears.

Fergus was so pleased and excited, he began to run round in circles, trying to catch his own tail.

Alison laughed. "Maybe it won't be so bad staying here after all," she whispered, picking the puppy up and hugging him.

"Of course it won't!" Fergus yapped, smothering Alison's face with huge wet licks. "We'll have lots of fun together! You'll see!"

Chapter Three

"The taxi's here!" Lauren yelled, as a black cab turned into the driveway.

"At last!" Rod hurried into the hallway, and glanced anxiously at the clock. "I hope I'm not going to be late."

Fergus began to whine. He

knew that it was time for his owner to leave, and he couldn't help feeling sad, even though he had so many new friends to look after him.

"I'll miss you, boy," Rod said, as he gave his puppy a big hug. "Be good!"

"I wish you weren't going," Fergus woofed sadly, as Rod ruffled the thick fur on Fergus's neck one last time, then gave him to Alison.

"Fergus seems to have taken a real shine to you, Ali," Rod said. "I know you'll take especially good care of him."

"Oh, I will!" Alison promised, her face lighting up.

"Can we bring Fergus outside to

say goodbye to you, Uncle Rod?"
Sarah asked, as the taxi driver
came to the door to collect the
suitcases.

"Yes, but put his lead on first,"
her uncle told her, handing it
over.

Alison put Fergus down, then
clipped the puppy's lead onto his
collar.

Fergus, meanwhile, had spotted
the taxi driver at the door. "Hello!"
he barked. "Another new friend!
Brilliant!"

"Fergus, what's the matter?"
Alison gasped, as the puppy
lunged towards the new arrival,
taking her with him.

"Oh, I forgot to warn you about
that!" Rod grinned, as Lauren,

Sarah and Mrs Grice burst out laughing. "Fergus is a *very* friendly puppy!"

"Hello, boy!" said the taxi driver cheerfully, squatting down to stroke Fergus.

"Hello!" Fergus snuffled eagerly round the man's shoes. "You're my friend now!"

"You'll be out for hours when you take Fergus for a walk," Rod warned them, as he climbed into the taxi. "He has to make friends with *everybody*!"

"Oh, he's so cute!" Lauren laughed, scratching the top of the puppy's head. "He seems to like *you* best, though, Ali."

Alison felt very proud as they all waved goodbye to Uncle Rod.

Fergus *did* seem to like her best. And now that she'd made friends with the puppy, she was quite looking forward to living at Uncle Rod's for the next month.

"Bye, Rod!" Fergus barked loudly as the taxi pulled away. "I'll miss you, but Alison will be my best friend while you're away!"

"Bye, Uncle Rod!" the girls shouted. They all followed the taxi to the bottom of the drive, and stood there, waving, as it sped off down the road.

Fergus didn't stop barking until the taxi was completely out of sight.

"Right, shall we unpack now?" Mrs Grice asked when they were inside again.

"Oh, Mum, do we *have* to?" Lauren groaned.

Mrs Grice smiled. "Well, I suppose we *are* on holiday! Shall we go shopping, and then have lunch somewhere?"

"Burgers!" Lauren yelled, running to get her jacket.

"No, pizza!" Sarah shouted, bouncing after her.

"Can Fergus come too, Mum?" Alison asked.

Mrs Grice shook her head. "Not if we're going to eat out, love. We'll take him for a long walk later."

Fergus began to whine miserably, but he cheered up when all three girls gave him a big hug before they left.

"Be good, Fergus," Alison whispered in his ear as she put him in his basket.

"Of course I will!" Fergus yapped. Then he yawned hugely. Actually, he *was* feeling rather tired. Maybe he would have a nap after all.

Two minutes later, as the front door banged shut behind Mrs

Grice and the girls, Fergus was
fast asleep . . .

Fergus was having a lovely
dream. He was running along a
sandy beach with Rod and Alison,
and they were throwing sticks for
him to chase. Then suddenly
there was a loud noise.

C-R-R-R-R-EAK!

Wide awake, Fergus jumped out
of his basket. He knew that noise!
It was the sound the big glass
doors in the living room made
when they were opened. Rod was
always saying he was going to do
something to stop the noise, but
he never did.

"Great!" Fergus yapped
excitedly. "That means Alison and

the others are back!" And he dashed out of the kitchen, skidding on the tiled floor. He couldn't *wait* to see his new friends again!

But as Fergus rushed into the living room, wagging his tail madly, he got a *very* big surprise.

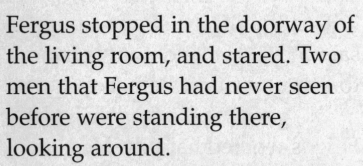

Chapter Four

Fergus stopped in the doorway of the living room, and stared. Two men that Fergus had never seen before were standing there, looking around.

"See? It wasn't difficult to get those French windows open, was it, Steve?" said the taller man. He held a big metal bar in his hand.

"Let's get started then, John," said the one called Steve.

"Hello, who are *you*?" Fergus woofed, wagging his tail. He trotted into the room. "Are we going to be friends?"

Both men jumped, and looked round.

"A dog!" muttered John. "Just our luck!"

"Don't panic, he's only a pup," said Steve. He held out his hand to Fergus. "Come here, boy."

"Oh, good. You *are* my friends!" Fergus woofed happily. He dashed across the room, sniffed at Steve's fingers, then rolled over to have his tummy tickled.

"He's really cute," said Steve. "I
wonder what breed he is?"

"Never mind that!" John
snapped. "What if he starts
barking? Someone might hear
him."

"All right, don't lose your cool!"
said Steve. "I bet this little
fellow's hungry, aren't you, boy?
Let's go and get some food."

"Oh, yes, please!" Fergus woofed happily, and gave Steve a quick lick.

John began to examine the silver candlesticks that stood on the mantelpiece.

"Be careful with those – they're Rod's favourites!" Fergus woofed, as he followed Steve into the kitchen.

Steve searched the cupboards until he found a box of dog biscuits. Then he filled Fergus's bowl right to the brim.

"Oh, great!" Fergus woofed, tail wagging. "Rod *never* lets me have this many all at once!" He began to tuck in straight away.

Steve patted Fergus then went over to the door. "Now you stay

here, boy, and eat those all up!"

"Thanks very much," Fergus
snuffled, through a mouthful
of biscuits. "See you in a
minute!"

But it took Fergus much longer
than that to polish off the whole
bowl. He had to keep having
drinks of water too, as the dry
biscuits made him thirsty.

When he had licked the crumbs from his bowl and had a final slurp of water, Fergus bounded eagerly over to the door to see his new friends again.

He was extremely disappointed to find that he was shut in. "Er . . . you shut me in by mistake, guys!" he woofed.

Nobody answered.

Fergus tried again. "Let me out, please!" he barked. But still, no one came.

Fergus listened hard by the door, but he couldn't hear anything. It sounded like his new friends had gone, without even saying goodbye.

Fergus sighed, then went over to his basket, climbed in, and settled down for another snooze.

A little while later, he bounced up again. The front door had opened, and he could hear the girls' voices. "Let me out, Alison!" he barked frantically. "Let me out!"

"Fergus!" The door opened and Mrs Grice and the girls came in.

Fergus flew at Alison, and jumped into her arms, tail wagging madly. "I've had a lovely time," he yapped happily. "Some more new friends came to visit!"

Alison was puzzled. "I don't remember shutting the kitchen door," she said to her mum.

Mrs Grice frowned as she picked up the box of dog biscuits on the worktop. "And we didn't leave that box out, did we?" she said.

But before she could say any more, there was a shout from Sarah, who'd gone into the study. "Mum! Uncle Rod's computer's gone!"

At the same moment, Lauren ran out of the living room. "Mum!" she gasped, "the French windows are open, and all Uncle Rod's silver candlesticks and bowls have gone too!"

Mrs Grice turned pale. "Oh no!" she groaned. "We've been burgled!"

"Burgled?" Fergus woofed. "What's that?"

"Poor Uncle Rod!" Alison said anxiously, hugging the puppy

close to her. "But thank goodness they didn't hurt Fergus!"

"Of course John and Steve didn't hurt me!" Fergus yapped cheerfully. "They were my friends!"

"I'll ring the police straight away," said Mrs Grice, hurrying to the phone.

"What's the police?" Fergus barked, puzzled. He just couldn't understand why everyone was looking so miserable.

But when Alison carried him into the living room, Fergus could see what they were talking about. "Where have all Rod's things gone?" he barked anxiously.

"Look! The video's gone as well." Lauren pointed at the

empty space under the TV.

"And that pretty gold clock from the mantelpiece," Sarah added.

Fergus stared from one person to another. "What's going on?" he whimpered.

"Oh, Fergus, why didn't you stop the burglars?" Sarah asked sadly.

"He couldn't have done anything," Alison said quickly. "He's only a puppy."

"The burglars must have given Fergus lots of food to keep him quiet," Mrs Grice said, still holding the box of dog biscuits. "It's not his fault."

"He probably made friends with them!" Lauren said, with a sad smile.

Fergus cowered in Alison's
arms. Now he knew he'd done
something very bad indeed.
Those two men, John and Steve,
hadn't been his friends at all.
They'd run off with Rod's things,
and Fergus hadn't even tried to
stop them. Rod was going to be
very upset, and it was all Fergus's
fault.

Chapter Five

Fergus whined softly. John and
Steve had come back to the house,
and they were taking Fergus's
favourite rubber bone. Fergus
wasn't going to let them get away
with it this time, though!
Growling, he ran after them and
grabbed Steve's ankle.

"Fergus? Are you awake?"

Fergus sat up, blinking in the early morning light. It was the day after the burglary, and the puppy was still feeling very bad about what had happened.

The police had come to the house to hear about the burglary, but they didn't know if they would be able to get all Rod's things back. That had made Fergus very unhappy. He hadn't wanted to sleep in his basket on his own that night, so he'd sneaked upstairs and onto Alison's bed.

"I can't sleep," Alison said, with a yawn. "Shall we get up, Fergus?"

Fergus didn't want to go back to

sleep either, because he kept having horrible dreams about the burglars. So he and Alison went quietly downstairs.

Mrs Grice was sitting at the kitchen table, having a cup of tea. She looked up, surprised, as Alison and Fergus came in. "Goodness me, you're up early!" she said.

"I couldn't sleep," Alison muttered.

"Neither could I," said Mrs Grice. She sighed. "Do you want some tea?"

Alison nodded.

"Mum!" Next minute Sarah appeared in her pink nightie, dragging her teddy with her. "I can't sleep."

"Shut up, Sarah!" Lauren's head appeared over the banisters. "What time is it, Mum?"

"Too early to be yelling like that!" said Mrs Grice. "Why don't you all go back to bed?"

"I keep thinking about the burglars." Sarah stuck her bottom lip out.

"Me too," Lauren added, coming down to join in.

Fergus gave a miserable little whimper. It was all *his* fault that everyone was awake early. Oh, if only he'd known that John and Steve weren't friends, after all!

Mrs Grice looked round at the four gloomy faces. "Tell you what," she said. "Let's have an early breakfast, and then go and find that car boot sale we saw advertised on the way here."

"What's a car boot sale?" Fergus woofed, but the three girls' faces lit up.

"Oh, cool!" Lauren exclaimed.

"Can we take Fergus, Mum?" Alison asked.

"Oh, please let me come!" Fergus whimpered. "I don't want to stay here in case John and Steve come back!"

Mrs Grice nodded. "Off you go and get dressed then," she said. "You have to get there early to get the best bargains!"

An hour later everyone, including Fergus, was in the car on their way to the boot sale. The puppy sat quietly on Alison's lap, watching the houses speed past. He still wasn't sure what a boot sale was, but anything was better than staying in the house on his own!

"I hope those burglars don't come back again!" Sarah remarked with a shiver.

"I'm sure they won't," said her mother firmly.

"Maybe Uncle Rod should get another puppy as well as Fergus," Lauren suggested. "Fergus is gorgeous, but he's a hopeless guard dog!"

Fergus whined unhappily. He didn't *want* Rod to get another puppy!

"Don't worry, Fergus," Alison whispered in his ear. "I'm sure you'll be a brilliant guard dog one day. You've just got to learn what to do, that's all!"

Fergus licked her nose gratefully. Next to Rod, Alison was his best friend.

The car boot sale was a lot further away than Mrs Grice had thought it was, and they had to check the map several times. But because they'd left home so early, they still arrived before many of the stallholders had unpacked their cars.

"Looks like there are lots of bargains to be had!" Mrs Grice said, as they began to walk up and down the rows of tightly packed cars with their goods on offer.

With Alison holding his lead, Fergus sniffed his way along, his ears pricking up. So *this* was a car boot sale! There were boxes lying on the ground, as well as tables piled high with clothes, books, plants and toys.

Fergus thought it was rather strange, but Alison and the others seemed to like it. Sarah bought a

cuddly panda. Then Alison
stopped to sort through a box of
story books.

At first, Fergus stood patiently
while Alison chose the books she
wanted. Then suddenly, he
smelled a very familiar smell. He
stiffened, sniffed the air again,
and turned to stare down the row
of stalls.

Yes, there they were, right in
front of him, unloading boxes
from an old white van. John and
Steve – the burglars!

Chapter Six

Fergus's ears went back, and he gave a low growl, deep in his throat. Those two men had taken Rod's things. And this time, Fergus was going to show them that he wasn't their friend at all!

"Wait a minute, Fergus," Alison said, as the puppy pulled on his lead. She was flicking through a story book wondering whether to buy it.

"I can't wait, Alison!" Fergus barked. He lunged forward, growling loudly. The book flew into the air as Alison was pulled after him.

"Fergus!" Alison gasped, turning bright red as everyone stared.

Fergus raced over to John and Steve, dragging Alison with him. The two burglars didn't notice the puppy. They were busy heaving a large box out of the van.

Quickly, Fergus began sniffing round the boxes John and Steve had already unloaded. Yes! This big box right here was full of

Rod's things! "It's *them*, Alison!" Fergus barked, scrabbling frantically at the box. "It's the burglars!"

"Fergus, stop it!" Alison gasped, trying to pull the puppy away. Everyone watching was laughing and pointing. Alison had never been so embarrassed in her life.

At that moment John and Steve turned round to see what was going on.

Fergus flattened his ears and bared his teeth. "You took Rod's things!" he growled. "Give them back."

"Fergus!" Alison said, horrified. "Stop that!"

Mrs Grice hurried over, with Lauren and Sarah. "Fergus! Come here!" she said sharply. "Alison, give me the lead."

"Look!" Fergus barked, scratching desperately at the box with Rod's things in it. "They're the burglars!"

The top of the box wasn't closed down properly, and suddenly Alison spotted a very familiar little gold clock inside. "Mum!" she gasped. "That looks like Uncle Rod's clock!"

Steve turned to John. "That's the pup from that big house yesterday!" he muttered. "Let's get out of here!"

The two men dashed off across the muddy field.

"Lauren, go and find one of the boot sale organisers," Mrs Grice

ordered, pulling out her mobile phone. "I'll ring the police."

Alison pulled the box open, while Fergus jumped up impatiently, trying to see inside. "Oh! All of Uncle Rod's stuff is here!" Alison exclaimed. She grabbed Fergus and swept him up into her arms. "Fergus, you're a hero!"

"Who's that? Don't let them in the house until I've checked them out!" growled Fergus, rushing down the hall as the doorbell rang.

"It's all right, Fergus!" Alison laughed as she picked the puppy up. "It's the police!"

But Fergus wasn't convinced

until Mrs Grice had opened the door, and he'd been properly introduced to PC Jones and PC Patel. Only then did he start wagging his tail.

"Did you find the burglars?" Sarah asked eagerly, as they all went into the living room.

PC Patel nodded. "It was easy to trace them, because in their panic at seeing Fergus, they'd left their van behind," she said. "Luckily, the car boot sale was too packed for them to make their getaway!"

"We arrested the two men a couple of hours ago," PC Jones went on. "And you'll be pleased to know that we found a lot of other people's stolen goods in the van as well. Now we can return it all to the rightful owners."

"That's wonderful!" Mrs Grice smiled. "I'll have some good news for Rod when I ring him!"

"Thanks to Fergus!" Alison added, giving the puppy a squeeze.

Fergus wagged his tail happily, and licked Alison's nose. Then his ears pricked up as he heard a noise outside. He jumped to his feet, and went over to the French windows to investigate.

"He's a great little guard dog!" said PC Jones admiringly.

Alison glanced at her mum and her sisters, and they all burst out laughing.

"Yes, he is – now!" Alison agreed.

"I can see you out there, Mr Blackbird!" Fergus barked, as he spotted a bird singing in the tree. "Just you be careful what you get up to in my owner's garden! I'm guarding everything, until Rod gets home. And though I'm still friendly, I can be really fierce – honest I can!"